For Lillian Moore, with thanks—A.T.

For Lise Winther—H.S.

First Edition   3 4 5 6 7 8 9 10

Library of Congress Cataloging in Publication Data
Tresselt, Alvin R.
The gift of the tree / by Alvin Tresselt ; illustrated by Henri Sorensen.
p.   cm. Summary: Traces the life cycle of an oak tree and describes the animals that depend on it for shelter and food. ISBN 0-688-10684-6.—ISBN 0-688-10685-4 (lib. bdg.)
1. Forest ecology—Juvenile literature.   2. Oak—Ecology—Juvenile literature.   [1. Oak.   2. Forest ecology.
3. Ecology.]   I. Sorensen, Henri, ill.   II. Title.   QH541.5.F6T74 1992 574.5'2642—dc20   90-20846   CIP   AC

ALVIN TRESSELT

The Gift of the Tree

ILLUSTRATED BY
HENRI SORENSEN

LOTHROP, LEE & SHEPARD BOOKS   NEW YORK

It stood tall in the forest.
For a hundred years or more the oak tree
had grown and spread its shade.

Birds nested in its shelter.
Squirrels made their homes in ragged bundles
of sticks and leaves held high in the branches.
And in the fall they garnered their winter food
from the rich rain of acorns
that fell from the tree.

Tucked under its gnarled roots, small creatures
found safety from the fox and owl.
Slowly, slowly, over the years the forest soil
increased as the brown, leathery leaves,
shaken down by the autumn winds,
moldered under the snow.

But even as the tree grew, life gnawed
at its heart. Carpenter ants tunneled through
the strength of the oak. Termites ate out
passageways in wondrous patterns.

A broken limb let the dusty spores of fungus
enter the heartwood of the tree.
And a rot spread inside the healthy bark.

Year by year the tree grew weaker
as its enemies worked.
Each spring fewer and fewer leaves unfolded,
and its great reaching branches turned gray with death.
Woodpeckers peppered the limbs with holes,
looking for the tasty grubs and beetles
that had tunneled the wood.
And here and there they dug bigger holes
to hold their babies.

In winter storms, one by one, the great branches
broke and crashed to the floor of the forest
until there remained only the proud trunk,
holding its broken arms up to the sky.

Now it was autumn, and the days were
long and lazy. Yellow-gray and misty mornings,
middays filled with false summer warmth,
and nights pierced with frost.

Then came a day of hurricane wind and slashing rain,
and as the fierce wind shrieked through the forest
the tree trunk split and crashed to the ground.
There it lay shattered, with only a jagged stump
to mark where it had stood for so long.

The cruel days of winter followed.
A family of deer mice settled into a hole
that had once held an arching branch.
A rabbit found protection from the biting wind
in the rotted center of the trunk.
And the ants and termites, the dormant grubs
and silent fungus, waited out the winter weather
under the bark and deep in the wood.

In the spring the young sun warmed the forest floor,
and acorns sprouted to replace the fallen giant.
Now new life took over the dead tree.
Old woodpecker holes made snug homes for chipmunks.
The hollow center of the trunk sheltered a family
of raccoons, while beneath the bark spread
the wood-eating fungus, ghost white and sulphur yellow.
And deep inside, the carpenter ants and the termites
continued their digging and eating.

On the trunk where the tree lay half buried
in the damp and musty leaf loam, the mosses stitched
a green carpet, softer than the softest wool.
Fragile ferns nestled in its shadow,
mushrooms popped out of the decaying mold,
and clumps of creamy white Indian pipes
clustered together, drawing nourishment
from the rich loam.

The years passed, and the hard wood grew soft and punky.
It crawled with a hundred thousand grubs and beetles.
Centipedes with their scrambling scurrying legs,
and snails and slugs all fed on the rotting wood.
And earthworms made their way through the feast,
helping to turn the tree once more into earth.
Pale shelf fungus clung to the sides like clusters of giant
clamshells, eating away and growing as the tree decayed.

A skunk came waddling by with her string of babies.
Sniffing at the wood, she ripped into its softness with her claws
to uncover the scrambling life inside, and eagerly
the family feasted. Secretive forest birds scratched and picked
for grubs and worms, pulling the tree apart bit by bit,
while the melting winter snows and soft spring rains
hastened the rotting of the wood.

And in this way, as new trees grew in strength
from acorns that had fallen long years ago,
the great oak returned to the earth.
On the ground there remained only a brown ghost
of richer loam where the proud tree had come to rest.